Ruby Rogers
Yeah, Whatever . . .

Sue Limb

Illustrations by Bernice Lum

BLOOMSBURY

First published in Great Britain in 2006 by Bloomsbury Publishing Plc
36 Soho Square, London, WID 3QY

Text copyright © Sue Limb 2006
Illustrations copyright © Bernice Lum 2006
The moral rights of the author and illustrator have been asserted

A CIP catalogue record of this book is available from the British Library

ISBN 0 7475 8322 6
9780747583226

All papers used by Bloomsbury Publishing are natural, recyclable
products made from wood grown in well-managed forests.
The manufacturing processes conform to the environmental
regulations of the country of origin.

Printed in Great Britain by Clays Ltd, St Ives Plc

1 3 5 7 9 10 8 6 4 2

www.bloomsbury.com
www.suelimbbooks.co.uk

Ruby Rogers
Yeah, Whatever . . .

CHAPTER 1
Don't be such an idiot, Ruby!

'T HIS IS MY FRIEND Ruby,' said
Yasmin to her granny.

'*Best* friend,' I whispered.

'Yeah, whatever . . .' said Yasmin. Her granny
got up out of her comfy chair, reached out and
grabbed both my cheeks. The old lady had some
grip. Her hands were like the jaws of a croco-
dile.

To say I was startled would be putting it mildly.
I almost screamed aloud in pain. Then the old dear
landed a smacking kiss on my forehead. Next, she

patted both my cheeks so hard that my teeth kind of rattled.

'Hey, call off your granny, will yah?' I muttered. 'While I still have a few brain cells left.'

Luckily Yasmin's granny doesn't speak much English. She doesn't live in England – this was just a visit – and she hasn't quite got the hang of how to be a granny in this country. Our grannies are a bit more chilled out. They don't inflict actual bodily injury when being friendly. Yasmin's granny was built like a rugby player. She towered over me. It was scary.

'Rubih!' she beamed and patted my cheeks again. 'Preetty baby!' To be honest, at this point she spat in my eye. I knew it wasn't deliberate, so I gracefully ignored it. She threw her arms around me and squeezed, hard.

'Tell her to cut all this baby stuff,' I gasped. 'Tell her I'm going to be a gangster when I grow up.'

'Don't be stupid, Ruby!' said Yasmin. 'Of course you're not.'

'I *so* am!' I hissed, kind of sideways out of the corner of my mouth. It was hard to face up to Yasmin while her granny had me in a wrestling hold.

Just then Yasmin's mum came over with a tray of

6

lovely warm honey cakes. Granny let go of me and we all sat down and started to guzzle. I love going round to Yasmin's after school. Her mum often bakes something specially for us. My mum's always at work till about five thirty, and even when she comes home, often she's too tired to cook.

'Ruby's family is very clever,' said Yasmin's mum to the granny. The granny looked blank, so she translated it for her. Mrs Saffet is a translator anyway. She works at home.

'Rubih!' cried the old lady. 'Iss family clebah!' And she did a weird little clapping kind of thing.

'Yasmin, show Granny the model Joe made,' said her mum.

My brother Joe hates his sculptures being called models, but I didn't say anything. Yasmin went over to the worktop where they have a few ornaments, a vase of flowers and Joe's sculpture. It's made of wood and it's on a kind of stand. You can't really tell if it's a bird or an aeroplane. Yasmin's granny sort of squinted at it and looked puzzled. She said something in Turkish. Yasmin's mum smiled and looked a bit embarrassed.

'She says is it a bird or a plane?' she said.

'You're not supposed to know,' I said. 'That's the point.'

'Granny's not really into modern art,' said Mrs Saffet, offering me another cake. The granny had stopped looking at Joe's sculpture and was mopping up her cake crumbs with her fingers.

I felt awkward. OK, my bro Joe is a total idiot and needs a complete make-over. In fact, it's top of my list of things to do. But I don't like it when people get tired of looking at his work after only five seconds. Ideally they should go on staring at it for weeks, drooling and fainting with joy.

'I think it's fabulous,' said Yasmin's mum. 'He's such a talented boy.'

Just then Zerrin arrived home. She's Yasmin's big sister. Her hair is long and black and shiny. She said hi to everybody and bent down and kissed her granny on the top of the head. Granny made a grab for her cheeks, but Zerrin managed to duck away, and as she escaped, she winked at me.

'Zerrin,' said her mum, 'show Granny that lovely photo of Joe's exhibition.'

Mrs Saffet is so polite. She was still hell-bent on telling Granny how wonderful my brother was. Zerrin went into the sitting room and came back with a big framed photo taken at the exhibition. The photo had been in the newspaper and Mrs Saffet had ordered a copy.

It was a photo of Joe, me, our mum and dad, Zerrin and her best friend Holly 'the Hellcat' Helvellyn, and Yasmin. Holly looked amazing with her make-up and everything. Joe had his eyes closed, the idiot. I looked like some kind of repulsive animal which lives in a hole in the desert. Zerrin and Yasmin looked beautiful and exotic – in fact, they stole the show.

Zerrin held out the photo to her granny, who took it and started to polish the glass with a corner of her skirt.

'Zerrin!' she said, pointing at the photo. '. . . Yasmin!'

'And that's Ruby, look!' said Mrs Saffet.

'Rubih!' said Granny, grinning at me.

'And that's Ruby's brother Joe!' said Mrs Saffet. 'He did all these models. Isn't he clever?' Granny nodded and went on polishing the glass. Then she pointed at Holly and said something in Turkish. Zerrin looked a bit tense, said something back and then took the photo away again.

'Granny doesn't like Holly much,' Yasmin told me later, when we were up in her room, arranging her dolls in rows. 'She doesn't like the way she's pierced her nose and everything. Holly came round last night and she had her Gothic stuff on and Granny started saying rude things – not in English, thank God.'

'Grown-ups don't realise just how cool Holly is,' I sighed. 'It's their loss. She's totally amazing. In fact, my project this term is to get her together with Joe. She clearly fancies him and he's just too stupid to ask her out. We've got to fix it up somehow. Let's make a plan. A brilliant plan!'

Yasmin fiddled with her dolls for a minute. I watched as she forced a miniature scrunchy over a doll's blonde hair and gave her a ponytail.

'Yasmin?' I said again.

'Yeah,' said Yasmin. 'Whatever. What name do you think I should give this doll? She used to be

Poppy but I've gone off that.' I was really annoyed. How could she could be more interested in her boring dolls than the real-life drama of my brother and the divine Holly 'the Hellcat' Helvellyn?

I buttoned my lip and stared out of the window. If Yasmin wasn't going to join in my plans for Joe and Holly, I certainly wasn't going to suggest any names for her stupid doll. In fact, Yasmin had been a bit irritating all day. I had the feeling we were on the verge of a really terrific row.

Yasmin loves rows, but I hate them. But when I'm at her house, I sort of have to be polite and go along with them. I decided I ought to suggest a name for the doll, after all – if only to avoid a row.

'Britney?' I suggested.

'Don't be such an idiot, Ruby!' snapped Yasmin. 'I've got two called Britney already.'

'Yeah,' I grumbled. 'Whatever . . .'

A row was certainly brewing. I had to think of something amazing to distract her. Yesss! A brilliant idea had whizzed into my head!

CHAPTER 2
We should have false names!

'HEY!' I SAID. 'I've thought of a brilliant idea! We should be a proper gang.'

'How can we be a gang with just two?' asked Yasmin.

'Well, we could start off with two, then maybe let other people in. If they're cool enough,' I said.

Yasmin just went on fiddling with her dolls. Unless I acted fast, we were in for an endless doll session. I hate doll sessions so much. I'd rather be rolled in coconut oil and sesame seeds and pecked at by birds all day.

'We could have a secret password,' I said. 'And we could have an initiation ceremony. We could have rituals and dares and secrets.'

Yasmin put her doll aside for a moment and twisted round to look at me. Her eyes were beginning to sparkle.

'We could be blood sisters!' she said. 'We could mingle our blood and sign our pact with it!' At this point I have to admit I almost fainted. I don't really like the sight of blood. It's top of the long list of things I'm afraid of, along with the dark, strange snarling dogs and waxworks. 'I'll go and get a needle!' said Yasmin and rushed out.

My heart was beginning to flutter. This was going to be my first gangsterish ceremony and I was going to disgrace myself by passing out – or possibly puking. Maybe both at once. I wished I'd never started this secret pact business. If only I could play with the dolls instead. I'd gladly sign up for a *whole week* of brushing the dolls' stupid hair and dressing them up for the dolls' stupid disco, as long as I didn't have to prick my finger and sign my name in blood.

The dolls stared at me and their blank faces seemed to be grinning in triumph. Yasmin came back in, looking disappointed.

'Mum won't let me have a needle,' she said. 'We'll have to use spit instead.'

I tried not to look too massively relieved. Yasmin got her felt tip pens and a piece of paper.

'OK,' she said. 'You write it – my handwriting's rubbish. What's it going to say in the pact thingy?'

'Our names,' I said. 'Our full names come first. *Ruby Emma Rogers* . . .' I wrote it down.

'No, we mustn't have our real names!' said Yasmin. 'We should have false names. Aliases.' I screwed up the sheet of paper and threw it away. Yasmin smoothed it out again and placed it in a cardboard box.

'We don't throw paper away like that, Ruby, you idiot!' she snapped. 'We recycle it, obviously.' She handed me a new piece.

'OK,' I said. 'Sorry, yeah. What's your false name going to be? Mine's Massive Deadly Poison Toad.'

'Mine's Diamond Monica,' said Yasmin. 'Write it down, write it down!'

I wrote:

Massive Deadly Poison Toad and Diamond Monica do hereby pledge allegiance to each other as blood sisters –

'*Spit* sisters,' said Yasmin. 'No, leave it. Spit sisters sounds stupid.'

They do promise to help their sister in whatever danger she be in. They do meet with secret handshake.

'What's the secret handshake?' said Yasmin. We tried a few out. First we bent down and shook hands back to back through our legs, but our bottoms collided. I lost my balance and toppled over.

'It's no good. It's not all that secret either,' said Yasmin. 'I mean, you'd only have to do it once in public and everybody would know what it was.'

'In fact, they'd be cracking up,' I agreed, rubbing my head. 'We've got to have a handshake that's secret but totally invisible to anybody watching . . . I know!'

'What?' said Yasmin, puzzled. I showed her what I meant. I grabbed her hand, and as I shook it, I kind of gently scratched the palm of her hand with my finger. She screamed and jumped away in fits of giggles.

'Can't have that!' she laughed. 'I'm ticklish!'

'OK, OK,' I said. 'How about this then?' I shook hands with her and quickly squeezed her hand hard, three times.

'Brilliant!' said Yasmin. 'Write it down!'

They do meet with secret handshake as agreed and secret password . . .

We stopped for a while and started to choose a password.

'Princess Barbie!'

'Chicago mob!'

'Chocolate hairslides!'

'Monkey business!'

In the end we decided to put Yasmin's sister's name together with my brother's name. Zerrin + Joe = Zerrijo. This was stylish, and fair, and it even sounded quite like a good name for a kitten.

Massive Deadly Poison Toad and Diamond Monica do promise to perform all rituals, keep all secrets and perform all dares as requested by each other. Hereby signed in spit.

'We ought to pretend it's blood, at least,' said Yasmin, getting out her paintbox. I changed the words to 'spit and blood'. Yas poked a bit of red paint out on to the bottom of the paper. We both spat on it and then she mixed it up with a paint-brush. It did look quite like blood. We signed it in paint and also with a red felt tip just in case the paint didn't work. Then we put it on her radiator to dry and solemnly shook hands.

'Zerrijo!' I said.

'Zerrijo!' replied Yasmin.

'OK, what's next?' I was really enjoying this. 'Secrets or dares?'

'Dares!' said Yasmin, and her eyes flashed in a way which I didn't quite like. A bit like an avenging goddess in the *World Religions* book at school. I was sure she was going to dare me to do something really appalling, even though she knows I'm the most scaredy of cats. I could win the Nobel Prize for Cowardice. But I screwed my face up, crossed my fingers and waited to hear my doom.

'In our silent reading lesson tomorrow,' she said, 'I dare you to make a farty noise.'

CHAPTER 3

It's got to be
something scary!

TERRIBLE FEAR SEIZED ME. I tried not to show it. Our teacher Mrs Jenkins is so fierce. She pounces on anybody who so much as moves during silent reading. Her hair is totally white and her eyebrows are utterly black. I sometimes think she might be a witch or a werewolf.

'Can't I have a different dare?' I asked, giving in to my terror. 'I mean, Jenko is . . . scary.'

'That's the point of a dare, you wuss!' said Yasmin. 'It's got to be something scary. Anyway, when you've done it, you can dare me to do something even more scary.'

This comforted me a bit. But for the whole of the rest of the evening I was worrying about silent reading tomorrow. And even when I was lying in bed that night, I was dreading it. When I finally drifted off to sleep, I dreamt I was being chased through a forest by a wolf who looked a bit like Mrs Jenkins.

'Wake up, Ruby!' Mum ripped off my duvet next morning. I tried to pretend I was too ill to go to school, but somehow Mum can always tell, and I didn't get very far with it.

'Come on, don't be such a wimp!' she said. 'It's drama club today, isn't it? You always love that!'

As she drove me to school I tried to focus on drama club. Silent reading was in the morning, and drama club was at lunchtime, so by then the dare would be over. It would be history.

'What's that little play you're working on, again?' asked Mum.

'It's burglars,' I said. It was a great play, actually. Mr Rivers who takes us for drama always divides us into pairs or threes. My partner is Dan Skinner. Dan's great. He's not very tall but he's quite strong, and he can make his eyes go all goggly and pull amazing faces just like a frog or a fish.

He invited me to his birthday party last year and it was a trip to the swimming pool. We had the best time imitating frogs and fish and stuff. I won a prize for my imitation of an octopus. He's one of my best mates and he calls me 'Rubix'. And I call him 'Froggo'.

I tried to concentrate on drama club, but first there was the dreadful ordeal of silent reading.

'Get your books out,' said Mrs Jenkins. Mine was *Bill's New Frock* by Anne Fine. It's a brilliant book but somehow I just couldn't concentrate on it. Everybody settled down and a huge, deep, prickling silence sprang up. Yasmin gave me a secret smile and raised her eyebrows slightly as if to say 'Get on with it!'

I knew I had to do a proper loud farty noise. Jenko was marking some books. Her head was bowed. She wouldn't see me. Now was the moment. I bowed my head too, as if I was reading. I put my tongue between my teeth and blew a raspberry.

'Fwwwwwwarp!'

A shocked giggle whizzed round the class like wildfire. Mrs Jenkins looked up and scowled.

'Quiet!' she barked. She stared in my general direction. 'Jason Gordon, was that you?' she snapped, glaring at the boy next to me.

'It wasn't me, miss!' he protested.

'Come out here to me!' boomed Jenko. Jason scrambled to his feet, but he didn't move in her direction. Who would?

'It wasn't me, honest, miss! It was Ruby Rogers!' Jason looked accusingly at me. Mrs Jenkins' awful eyes turned on me, and I felt my face boil as a huge blush broke out.

'Is that right, Ruby?' demanded Jenko. 'Was it you?'

I hesitated. I couldn't deny it. Everybody sitting round me knew it was me. They were all looking at me and trying to hide their grins. Dan even turned round and secretly gave me the thumbs-up sign. No way could I deny it.

'I'm sorry, miss,' I said. 'I couldn't control myself.'

'Stay behind afterwards,' said Jenko sternly. 'You can spend the lunch hour On Punishment.'

'But it's drama club, miss!' I protested.

'Not for you it isn't,' said Jenko. 'Not today.'

I was horrified. Just one little silly noise and now I was going to miss my beloved drama club, the highlight of my week.

'Settle down now,' said Mrs Jenkins, 'and if anybody else wants to be silly, they'll be On Punishment at lunchtime too.'

Yasmin was sitting across from me with her back to Mrs Jenkins, and she gave me a huge grin as if to congratulate me on my superb dare. I didn't grin back, though. I was miserable at the thought of missing drama club and having to stand outside the head's office for the whole lunch hour instead. And Mrs Jenkins might even send a letter home to my mum and dad! How had I got into this mess? I couldn't help feeling it was all Yasmin's fault somehow.

CHAPTER 4
You're just a total loser

AFTER GRABBING A QUICK lunch, instead of going to drama club I had to go to the lobby, where Mrs Jenkins was waiting.

'Right,' she said briskly. 'You stand here, hands by your sides, until the bell goes. That's forty minutes. You don't speak to anyone, and at the end of the time I shall come back and we'll go in to Mrs Wakefield and you'll apologise.' I nodded, trying to look saintly while secretly shaking with fear.

Mrs Wakefield's the head teacher and she can be

even more scary than Jenko. She's tall and fat and pale and she can be really icy and sarcastic.

I took up my position just to the right of her door. I could see the lobby clock from there and it seemed an awful long way for the fingers to go: right round from one o'clock to a quarter to two. How boring was this?

But wait! There was something to watch, in fact. The swing doors to the hall open into the lobby, and they're glass doors, so I could see into the hall where drama club was in full swing. It wasn't very noisy, although drama club sometimes is. But of course everybody was practising their burglars plays. Everybody except me.

Suddenly I saw Yasmin. She was obviously being the burglar – I saw her mime opening a window and climbing in. Then she was creeping about. Yasmin's good at drama, I have to admit. She tip-toed towards her partner, who was lying on the floor 'asleep'. She mimed opening a drawer in a bedside cupboard, and he woke up. He jumped up – and horror! It was Dan Skinner! Dan was supposed to be my partner! We'd rehearsed our burglar play soooo many times, and now Yasmin had stolen him!

They did a slow-motion fight, just like the one

Dan and I had worked out. I could only stand and watch. I felt sort of mad with jealousy. Then Mr Rivers asked everybody to stop rehearsing and sit down. Now it was time for the various pairs to show their plays. And guess which pair he picked first? Yasmin and Dan, of course!

'Yasmin and Dan have added something really exciting to their play,' said Mr Rivers. 'Look carefully at what happens when Dan wakes up.' When Yasmin and Dan performed their play again, they had to do it in a slightly different place in the hall, and I couldn't see them. All I could see was Mr Rivers watching them. He was grinning like anything.

When their play ended, there was a huge burst of clapping. Mr Rivers joined in. He's a really lovely teacher and he's young and gorgeous too, in an Orlando Bloom kind of way.

'Well done, Yasmin and Dan!' he said. 'Now can any of you tell me what was special about that?'

Somebody answered in a mumble. I couldn't hear.

'Yes, that slow-motion fight scene at the end was amazing!' said Mr Rivers. 'I've seen professional actors do fights that weren't as good as that. Brilliant! Well done, the pair of you. Now let's see Max and Hannah.'

I turned round to face the wall. I didn't want to see any more. I didn't want to hear any more either. I could have been in that hall, having fun and getting praised to the skies by wonderful Mr Rivers. And instead I was stuck here in disgrace.

I did what I always do when I have to get through something. I closed my eyes and imagined I was living in a tree house in the rainforest with my monkeys Stinker, Funky and Hewitt. Boy, was I going to have a big cry when I got home.

Eventually, after what seemed like three years, the bell went and Mrs Jenkins appeared. Mrs Wakefield was with her. We all went into Mrs

Wakefield's study and shut the door. It seemed very solemn in there. Mrs Wakefield didn't sit down. She went round and stood behind her desk and stared down at me.

'And why were you On Punishment, Ruby?' she asked in a churchy sort of voice.

'Please, miss, I made a noise in silent reading,' I said.

'Ruby disturbed the class and deliberately destroyed the atmosphere,' said Mrs Jenkins. 'In a silly and rude way.'

'If I ever see you standing here in disgrace again,' said Mrs Wakefield, 'you'll be in serious trouble, and I'll have to ask your parents to come in and have a talk. Is that clear?'

I nodded. A horrible cold feeling ran up the backs of my legs at the thought of my parents coming in, looking all embarrassed and shocked.

'You will apologise to Mrs Jenkins,' said Mrs Wakefield.

'I'm very sorry,' I said.

'Right then. You may go. And remember what I said,' said Mrs Wakefield, and she stared down at me and flared her eyes so they looked quite savage. I backed off. Mrs Jenkins opened the door for me and we walked back to the classroom. All my mates were in there making a noise. It seemed like a happy blur. How I wished I was part of it.

'Sit here, Ruby, down at the front,' said Mrs Jenkins. I obeyed. Everybody else quietened down and Jenko took the register. Then we started the lesson. It was maths. I couldn't concentrate and I made a complete mess of it. In maths Mrs Jenkins always walks around the room helping people, and while she was busy with Fiona Kennedy I turned round just to have a quick look for Yasmin. Maybe she would reward me with a supportive smile.

Over at the back of the classroom, Yasmin was sitting between Dan and Hannah, but she didn't look up. It all seemed very cosy. I couldn't wait for the bell to go so we could be reunited and she could tell me how wonderfully daring I had been.

At last the bell went and we gave in our work and packed up our things. I went over to where Yasmin was whispering something in Dan's ear. They were both giggling.

'So, what did you think of my dare?' I asked.

'What?' said Yasmin absent-mindedly, as if I'd interrupted her really enjoyable conversation with Dan. 'Oh, yeah, brilliant. Whatever.'

'It's time for your dare now,' I said. 'I dare you to

walk all the way home with your bum stuck out like a duck. Sort of waddling.'

'Oh, I can't do that, Ruby,' said Yasmin, sounding busy and important. 'Not today. Sorry. I'm going home to have tea with Dan. His mum's coming to collect us in her new four-by-four. See you tomorrow!'

And Yasmin actually pushed past me and went off with Dan. He said something I didn't hear and she burst out laughing. I couldn't help thinking it was something about me. But I wasn't going to get upset. I was just going to walk home by myself. Or maybe I'd walk as far as the high school and wait for Joe to come out. Things were completely OK.

As I walked out of school, though, a huge tear appeared from nowhere and ran down my cheek. I rubbed it away. Stupid blinking tears! A little voice in my head seemed to be jeering at me. 'Well, that was a triumph, wasn't it? Could any day possibly have been worse? And it was all your own fault – you're just a total loser.'

CHAPTER 5

Luminous green hair and snake sandwiches!

I WALKED ON, STARING DOWN at the pavement so nobody would see my face. Just in case a few more tears appeared from nowhere. Then I saw a pair of really cool boots barring my way. They were lace-up ones with buckles on, like women's motorcycling boots.

'Not so fast,' said a menacing voice. I looked up. It was Holly! Holly 'the Hellcat' Helvellyn! She was looking super-cool in a lop-sided skirt (long on one side and short on the other) and a fluffy mohair jumper in black and red stripes. She's in the sixth form now, and they can wear what they like.

'Ruby!' her grin faded. 'What's the matter, babe? C'mon, spill the beans. Tell Auntie Holly all about it.' She turned to walk with me and wound my arm round hers. I told her the whole thing, finishing with Yasmin refusing to do my dare and waltzing off to have tea with Dan.

'Just wait till I see her next!' said Holly. 'I'll give her a talking-to! Never mind, Ruby. Dare me to do something instead. And make it really, really terrifying.' She looked down at me and winked merrily. She was so fantastic.

I thought for a moment. What I really wanted more than anything was for Holly to stay with me for ages and ages.

'I dare you to come home and have tea with me,' I said. Holly pretended to be horrified.

'Oh no!' she gasped. 'Not . . . tea at the crumbling old Rogers' mansion! With your cobweb-festooned dad coming out of the wardrobe the moment the sun sets! And your mum with her luminous green hair and snake sandwiches!'

'And Joe?' I said. I wanted to see if Holly showed

31

any signs of still fancying Joe. I was sure she had the hots for him, but the stupid boy just didn't seem to notice.

'And your vile brother Joe, of course,' said Holly, squeezing my arm tightly. 'With that horrid bolt through his neck, and his vampire teeth, and his garland of small rodent skulls . . . Urghhhhhhhhhh!' she shuddered. 'OK then. I know I can't refuse a dare or you'll know what a great big cowardy wuss I am in secret. Lead me on to your haunted dungeons!'

When we arrived home, nobody else was about. Mum and Dad usually come home around five. I was so hoping Joe had come home early.

'So . . .' I said. 'Would you like a cup of tea? Would you mind putting the kettle on? The switch is a bit too high for me.'

Holly obliged. She also found the breadbin and made us each a couple of slices of toast. I didn't have tea, though. I had Fair Trade Mango Orange and Passion Fruit juice.

'Hmm,' said Holly, reading the side of the carton. 'Glad to see you're supporting this man who grows passion fruit in Honduras. Thanks to you, he can afford to send his kids to school!' I felt pleased, although I didn't completely understand how it worked.

'Will you put that in writing?' I said. 'I could show it to Jenko tomorrow and then she would realise that I'm not a she-devil after all.'

'It would be quite nice to pretend to be a she-devil sometimes, though,' said Holly thoughtfully. 'When you've finished that last piece of toast, I'll do you a face-painting job if you like. She-devil, tiger or monkey? The choice is yours.'

I was so glad Holly wasn't going to rush off. I was longing for Joe to come home and be nice to her. So I took a long time clearing away the tea things and loading and re-loading the dishwasher, while Holly got her face-paints out.

'I never travel without a truckload of make-up,' she confessed, unpacking her silver metallic case. 'Homework, almost nothing. A few milligrams or whatever. Make-up, five tonnes. Now what's it going to be?'

'A tiger!' I said. 'No, wait – a monkey.'

'Tell you what,' said Holly. 'I'll do you a monkey face first and then I'll take a photo of you with my mobile. Then we'll clean the monkey off and do you a tiger face for afters.'

It seemed Holly didn't mind how long she

stayed. When was Joe going to show? He was really, really late, the idiot.

Holly designed a perfect monkey face for me, and then we went upstairs and she took some photos of me with my toy monkeys, in my tree-house bedroom.

'Weirdly lifelike,' said Holly. 'I'll e-mail you a copy and we can print it out and frame it.'

Just then we heard the front door open downstairs and somebody come in. It was still a bit early for Mum or Dad to come home, so it had to be Joe. Or a burglar.

'Joe!' I ran out on to the landing and peeped down over the bannisters. Joe looked up.

'Schoolboy Finds Ape in House,' he said, chucking his schoolbag in a corner. Joe often talks in newspaper headlines. '"I Was Alerted by Terrible Stench," He Says.'

'Holly's here,' I said. Holly came up beside me and looked down too. Joe looked up at her and his face kind of changed slightly. He didn't look particularly pleased to see her. Just slightly on edge.

'Oh, hi,' he said.

'Hi, Rogers,' said Holly. 'How's life?'

'Oh, tragic and meaningless,' said Joe.

'Ruby's had a horrible day,' said Holly. 'So I came back with her to cheer her up.'

'Schoolgirl Has Unpleasant Day,' said Joe. 'Shock Horror.' And then he just walked off into the kitchen! How rude! Right in the middle of talking to Holly. I was going to have to work miracles to get them together. Starting right now.

CHAPTER 6

It's one of the worst days ever

I RACED DOWNSTAIRS AND into the kitchen. Joe was getting a can of drink out of the fridge.

'Let's have some nachos with cheese and beans!' I said. I know Joe adores nachos. He would probably say yes to nachos even if he had to sit and eat them with somebody really horrid. Even a zombie or something. So the combination of nachos and the divine Holly would be a homecoming straight from heaven.

I switched the oven on. Joe was leafing through a magazine lying on the table – it was Holly's magazine, full of celeb gossip. Holly came into the kitchen.

'There's a brilliant feature on celebs with their eyes shut and their mouths open in there,' said Holly. 'It's towards the end.' She stood quite close to Joe and helped him find the place.

Wow! This was going brilliantly! Already they were hardly aware I was in the room!

'Just going to the loo,' I said and whizzed upstairs. In the bathroom, I wondered if I should just stay upstairs for a while and let them stare into each other's eyes down there. Maybe I should not go downstairs again, ever. I wasn't sure. I used up a bit of time by cleaning my fingernails with the nailbrush. I don't think I've *ever* done that before. They looked rather magnificent.

Then, suddenly, I heard a strange and awful noise. Joe came upstairs, went into his bedroom and shut the door with a horrid final sound! Moments later his loud music broke out. What was he doing up here, the idiot? He should be down in the kitchen with Holly!

I rushed out of the bathroom and raced downstairs. Holly was packing up her make-up stuff and looking slightly annoyed. She was a bit pink and her lips seemed kind of tightly shut.

'Where's Joe gone?' I said. 'Let's get those nachos on! They're his favourite!'

'He said he had to check his e-mails,' said Holly with a sort of shrug. 'I'm sorry, Ruby, I don't think I can stay for the nachos. I've just realised how late it is. I've got to get home.'

'But you said you'd give me a tiger face!' I said, dismayed.

'I know. I'm sorry. Next time, OK? Do you want me to take the monkey face off now, or keep it on?'

'Keep it on,' I said.

'OK,' said Holly. 'I'll leave you some cotton wool balls and cold cream to take it off with . . .' She put these items on a plate and then zipped up her bag. She was all packed and ready to leave. My heart nearly shattered into a million pieces. It had all gone so horribly wrong.

'Bye, babe,' she said and bent down and gave me a hug. 'See you soon.'

'Bye,' I said sadly. 'And thanks for cheering me up.'

Neither of us said anything about Joe going upstairs and shutting his door and putting on his

38

music. But we both knew he'd kind of ruined everything.

After Holly had gone, I wondered what to do. I knew I shouldn't run upstairs and bang on Joe's door and tell him off for being rude to Holly. You have to be really subtle and tactful when it comes to these boy/girl things. I just sat in the kitchen and drew spiders' webs on my hand.

After about ten minutes, Joe's music stopped and he came down. He was wearing different stuff and he smelt nice.

'Where's what's-her-name?' he asked.

'She's gone,' I said. Joe pulled a face and shrugged. He was trying to look as if he didn't give a flying

fandango but I knew (or hoped, anyway) that he was really cross.

'Whatever,' he said. It seemed a useful word. 'Where are those nachos, then?' He glared at the oven. It was on, but empty. I got up and switched it off. The fan stopped with a sad kind of groan.

'I didn't think there was any point in having nachos if Holly wasn't staying,' I said and picked up my schoolbag. 'I'm going to do my homework.'

I trailed upstairs and shut myself in my room. I climbed up into my tree-house bed and lay down miserably with my monkeys.

'Funky, Stinker, Hewitt,' I said. 'Today sucks. It's one of the worst days ever.'

'Play tennis,' suggested Hewitt. He had to say that, because he's holding a tennis racket. 'That should cheer you up.'

'Eat something,' said Stinker, patting his enormous tummy. 'I recommend bananas, or possibly the leaves of the pollokki-wolloki tree.'

'Bend my legs back behind my head and tie me in a knot,' offered Funky. 'Go on, feel free. It won't hurt at all, I promise.'

But in the end I just read a chapter of my book. It was a history book about life in the year 1500. Apparently most princesses were married off to princes in those days. Most people had arranged marriages. However did they manage to organise it? I couldn't even get my two to have some nachos together.

Eventually I heard Mum come in, and I ran downstairs to give her a hug. She looked startled as I bounded into the kitchen.

'OOOOh, Ruby, you made me jump!' she said. 'Who did that lovely monkey face for you? Was it Joe?'

'No, it was Holly,' I said. 'She walked home with me because I'd had a bad day.'

'What sort of bad day?' asked Mum. 'Trouble at school, was it?'

'No, no!' I said hastily. I didn't want her to know I'd been On Punishment for the whole of the lunch hour. 'It's just that Yasmin went off with some other people today, and I think she likes Dan more than me.'

'Rubbish!' said Mum. 'And even if she does, never mind. There's plenty more fish in the sea.'

'Holly made me feel better,' I said. 'Can she babysit for me next time you go out?'

'Joe can babysit for you, love,' said Mum.

'Joe's useless,' I said. 'Last time you told him to babysit, he just went out at half past eight with his friends and he didn't come back till eleven. Please let Holly babysit for me! Oh please!'

'Oh, all right then,' said Mum with a sigh. 'She's a very talented girl.' Mum used to diss Holly because of her Gothic clothes. But now she likes her. Ever since Holly's mum put on an exhibition of Joe's work in her gallery, Holly's been No 1 on Mum's hit parade. 'We're going out this Saturday, as a matter of fact. It's Dr Harris's retirement party. They're having a big posh dinner dance at the Royal Oak Hotel.'

'I'll ask Holly if she can come,' I said. I whizzed her a text there and then. If only I could get Holly and Joe in the same room together for half an hour, I was sure they'd click. I knew now that Joe had gone upstairs to get changed and try and look – and smell – nicer. So he must really like Holly after all. Holly sent a text back right away, saying she'd be delighted to babysit. Right! This time it just had to work!

The phone rang. Mum picked it up. At the same time Dad arrived, and Joe's music stopped and he came downstairs.

'Phone call for you, Ruby,' said Mum, holding it out for me. 'It's Yasmin.'

'Yes!' I said. 'Hi!'

'Hi, Ruby!' said Yasmin. She sounded a little strange. 'I just wanted to say I'm sorry if I upset you today, you know, and stuff.'

'Oh, no,' I said, shrugging. 'I'm fine.'

'I mean, I'm sorry I had to work with Dan in drama club,' said Yasmin, 'but Mr Rivers told me to, because Billy was away too. And I'm sorry I went off to have tea with Dan, but when he asked me I thought it would be rude to say no.'

'It's fine,' I said. 'Whatever!' What a useful word it was. It was kind of accepting stuff, but still being just a tiny bit rude underneath. Like pulling a face at somebody behind their back.

'Holly rang Zerrin just now and told her you

were really upset on the way home,' Yasmin went on. So this apology was all because Holly had been nice and stuck up for me again! I so had to fix her up with my brother. Otherwise, life just wasn't fair.

'I was a bit upset,' I said, 'but it wasn't because of you and Dan. I saw a cat that had been run over.'

'Ugh!' said Yasmin. 'Was it completely squashed and dead?'

'Yeah,' I sighed. 'Whatever.'

'Anyway,' Yasmin dived back into the main conversation, 'will it be OK if Dan joins our gang? Only I sort of promised him he could and I said he could do the initiation ceremony tomorrow lunchtime.'

A thunderbolt of anger flashed through me. OK, I like Dan better than any other boy in the class. He's my best boy mate. He's special. He's funny. But Yasmin had gone and said he could join our gang without even asking me! I began to wish she'd never rung up after all.

'Yeah, whatever,' I said, in a grumpy sort of voice. 'See you tomorrow, then. I've got to go now. Bye.'

I rang off. Mum was getting food out of the fridge. Dad was listening to voicemail messages. Joe was sitting at the table looking bored.

'Monkey Has Difficult Day at the Office,' he said. 'Bananas Over-Ripe and Fleas Biting Harder Than Usual.'

I could hit him sometimes.

CHAPTER 7

I've already had
enough of your silliness

NEXT DAY AT SCHOOL it was art in the morning. I love art. Although, to be honest, I'm rubbish at it. Yasmin and I bagged the best table – the cosy one by the radiator. Yasmin plonked her bag down on one of the other chairs.

'I'll save that for Dan,' she said. 'Dan! Come over here!'

Dan came over with his friend Max, who is a tall thin boy. His ears stick out and he doesn't say much, but he can make a noise that sounds just like a swarm of bees attacking a very small horse. This can be helpful when we're trying to get through a rainy lunch hour. There was just one other chair left.

'Let's get Hannah over here!' said Yasmin. 'She's so funny!'

I felt annoyed. I'm the one who'd supposed to be funny. OK, I know Hannah gets the giggles easily, but that hardly counts as *being* funny.

Hannah came over and joined us. She has very long hair and she's got an irritating habit of flicking it back over her shoulders. She came up, sat down, and right away she flicked back her hair and it whipped into my eye. It stung like mad.

'Ow!' I cried.

'Ruby Rogers!' said Mrs Jenkins in her stern voice. 'I've already had enough of your silliness this week!'

'I'm sorry, miss,' I said, 'but Hannah hit me with her hair.' Everybody laughed. This was awful. I didn't mean it to sound funny, but it somehow did.

'Ruby, you can come down and sit here by me,' said Mrs Jenkins. 'I'm not having any more of your stupidity.' I got up, collected my things and went down to sit at the small desk next to Mrs Jenkins' teacher's table.

'Right!' said Mrs Jenkins. 'Today we're going to do portraits. You're going to paint a picture of the person sitting next to you.' It was handy that I was in disgrace again, then. Hannah would be Yasmin's partner and Dan would paint Max. A perfect stinking foursome.

'Has anybody not got a partner?' asked Mrs Jenkins. I put my hand up. 'Oh, Ruby. Well, you'll just have to do a self-portrait.'

We all started painting. I dipped my brush in brown paint and did a big oval shape for my head. People were chatting and giggling. Mrs Jenkins lets us talk quietly in art. Anyway, it would be impossible to paint somebody's portrait without talking to them just a little bit. I felt depressed. All around me people were enjoying themselves, but I was banished to the loser's desk just for saying 'ow' when something hurt. I drew in two sad black eyebrows.

'You've got such lovely long hair, Hannah!' said Yasmin. I could hear her voice above the general hum.

'You've got lovely long hair too, Yas!' said Hannah. I gritted my teeth. They sounded gross, drooling over each other's hair. I think it's called a mutual admiration society. My hair is short and messy. I painted in a few short scrappy spikes of hair on my self-portrait. Maybe if I grew my hair Yasmin would prefer me to Hannah. I would start growing it right now. Maybe if I really concentrated, it would be down to my shoulders by lunchtime.

'You've got some lovely nits in your lovely long hair, Yas,' said Dan. Hannah giggled.

'Shut up, Froggo!' said Yasmin. 'Anyway, your dog has fleas.'

'Your *dad* has fleas,' said Dan.

'Yes, but they are the very *best* fleas,' said Yasmin.

They were all giggling. Why didn't Mrs Jenkins tell them off? They were having a ball without me. It didn't seem to matter to them at all whether I was there or not. Yasmin was even calling Dan 'Froggo', for goodness' sake. That was *my* name for him. *I* was the one who had thought of it. She'd never called Dan 'Froggo' before yesterday, when she'd gone home and had tea with him.

I painted in a mouth for myself. It looked a bit cross. I wasn't sure how to do the nose, so I just did two dots for the nostrils. Then I did the eyes. I couldn't get them to match. One of them was small and slitty and the other was big and tilted and alarming. I looked like an alien.

A shadow fell across my desk. Mrs Jenkins was standing next to me. I tried not to cringe.

'I think you've been a bit hard on yourself, Ruby,' she said. 'You're not that bad-looking. Make those lips curve upwards at the edges. There's no need to make yourself look so grim.'

No need to look grim? How could she say that? I had so many reasons to look grim. First of all, Jenko herself. She clearly had it in for me. Then Yasmin, who seemed to like Dan and Hannah a lot more than she liked me. And there was always that hopeless project to get my loser brother to be nice to Holly.

I got some red paint and sort of curved the edges of my mouth upwards, but it didn't look very jolly. It looked like somebody trying to smile while secretly, inside, they were kind of sad and furious. A very lifelike portrait, then.

Ruby Rogers

CHAPTER 8
Don't you call me an idiot!

AT LUNCHTIME, AFTER a pizza and some squash, Yasmin and I went out to the schoolyard, by the boiler room wall. It's a nice warm little corner there.

'I told Froggo to come,' said Yasmin. 'And Hannah. I said she could be in our gang too. She's got such lovely hair.'

'What's hair got to do with it?' I complained. 'If it's nice long shiny hair that matters, you might just as well never bother to speak to me again! Mine's like a bird's nest!'

'Don't be so stupid, Ruby,' said Yasmin. 'Hannah's funny. That's why I like her.'

'Funnier than me?' I demanded angrily. Yasmin stared at me, looking quite surprised.

'No, not funnier than you, you idiot,' she said. 'But just because you're funny doesn't mean that nobody else is allowed to be funny!'

'Don't you call me an idiot!' I snapped. 'And before you invite people into our gang, maybe you should ask me what I think! It's not your gang! It was my idea!'

'It so was NOT!' said Yasmin fiercely.

It was at this point that Dan and Hannah arrived. They could see we were kind of having a row.

'Can we join your gang now?' said Hannah, flicking her hair about again.

'Never mind the gang!' grinned Dan. 'Can we join in your row?'

'You can't join the gang now,' I said. 'To join you have to sign the pact and we haven't got any paper or anything.'

'We don't need paper, Ruby!' said Yasmin bossily. 'Froggo and Han can just say their promises and they can sign the paper later. They can learn the password and the secret handshake now.'

'Great!' said Hannah. 'I love secret handshakes!'

'I prefer secret milkshakes,' said Dan. 'But maybe we can have some of those later too. Hey! Let's have special gang food that's revolting, but we have to eat it without gagging to prove we're hard.'

'Don't you start telling us how our gang has got to be!' I said angrily. I really like Dan, but he was starting to try and run the show and he wasn't even a member yet. I didn't like the thought of having to eat revolting food anyway. It was a typical boy's idea.

'OK,' said Yasmin. 'You've got to promise to – what was it, Ruby?'

'Do you promise to perform all rituals, keep all secrets, and perform all dares as requested by each other?' I said rather crossly.

'I do,' said Dan. 'Hey! It's like getting married.'

'I will,' said Hannah, giggling.

'I now pronounce you gang members,' said Yasmin.

'Wait!' I said. 'They've got to have special gangster names.'

'Oh yes!' said Yasmin. 'I forgot. Ruby's Massive Deadly Poison Toad and I'm Diamond Monica.'

'I'll be Plate of Sick,' said Dan.

'I'll be Priscilla,' said Hannah.

'You can't be Plate of Sick,' I said. 'It's too revolting. Anyway, it's not gangsterish enough. Nor is Priscilla. You just sound like a Barbie doll.'

'I'll be Murder Mick, then,' said Dan. 'It rhymes with Plate of Sick.'

'I'll be Thriller Priscilla,' said Hannah.

'OK, now for the handshake,' said Yasmin. 'I'll secretly give Dan the handshake and Ruby can give it to Hannah.'

Typical! I wanted to give Dan the secret handshake and Yasmin had bagged him again. I gave Hannah the three secret squeezes. In fact, I gave

her the hardest squeezes I could manage, and she yelped a bit. It was payback time for her hitting me with her hair.

'No need to overdo it, Ruby!' said Yasmin. 'If you do it so hard it hurts, it can't be a secret any more, can it?'

'Now tell us the password!' said Dan.

'It's Zerrijo,' said Yasmin. 'It's a mixture of my sister's name – Zerrin – with Ruby's brother's name – Joe.'

'If we're joining the gang, we should have our brothers' and sisters' names in the password too,' said Dan.

'I haven't got any brothers and sisters,' said Hannah. 'So maybe we could put my dad's name in? He's called Craig.'

'No!' I said. 'The password stays the same!' I hated the way they were moving in and taking over. Right now I could happily have kicked them both, with one leg each, except I'd have fallen over. Life is so difficult sometimes.

'No, Ruby!' said Yasmin. 'It's not really fair. Now we're a gang of four I think we should change the password. In fact, we should change it every time we get new members.'

'How many more members are you planning to

invite?' I snapped. 'Fifty? Some long password that would be!'

'Well, my brother's Matthew,' said Dan. 'So the password could be Zerrijomatt.'

'Or Zerrimattjo,' said Hannah.

'Or Mattjozerri,' said Yasmin. They all laughed. They were being so stupid. It seemed to me they were just making fun of our gang and it didn't have its secret glamour any more.

'We don't have to use the "Matt" bit,' I sneered. 'We could use "hew". And since Hannah's not got a brother or sister, we could use a bit of her name. So why don't we make it Zerrijo-hew-hah!' I'd meant it as a really sarcastic kind of comment, but to my astonishment, they all cheered and clapped.

'Brilliant!' said Dan.

'Ruby! You're a genius!' said Yasmin.

'Zerrijo-hew-hah!' yelled Hannah, jumping up and down and flicking her dangerous hair all over the place. 'This is going to be the best gang ever!' They all seemed as pleased as punch.

I was the only one who felt the gang had lost all its secret magic. In fact, I was beginning to think I might just have to hand in my resignation. Yasmin had ruined our gang before it had even had a chance to get started. I was *so* tempted to go off on my own and form a secret gang of one.

CHAPTER 9

Stinker, I gotta problem

THAT EVENING MUM and Dad decided to reorganise their bedroom, so they were busy upstairs. Joe was lounging on the sofa watching some music videos. I was sitting on the floor playing with my Game Boy.

But I wasn't really concentrating. I couldn't stop thinking how wonderful it would be if Joe went out with Holly. She would come round all the time and be nice to me. In fact, she'd be extra-nice to me because I was Joe's sister. I peeped at Joe.

He was staring at the TV with his mouth slightly

open and a totally moronic expression on his face. His fingernails were filthy and his hands were covered with paint from his A level art coursework. He had kicked his shoes off in order to lie full length on the sofa, and his socks smelt utterly rank. Gross!

'Holly's coming to babysit on Saturday,' I said. 'Maybe we could have a feast. Those nachos we didn't get around to having last time.'

'Hhhhhuh,' said Joe, still staring at the telly. I was sure he wasn't listening.

'Joe?' I said.

'Yeah, whatever . . .' said Joe, his eyes still fixed on the screen.

'Joe, there's an alien looking in through the window,' I said. Joe didn't react.

'Uh-huh,' he said.

It was hopeless. But I wasn't going to get anywhere by dropping hints or talking about Holly anyway. That would only be a massive turn-off as far as Joe was concerned. I had to be clever. Perhaps it was just as well he hadn't been listening. Mentioning Holly like that was so obvious. I'd been stupid. I had to go back to square one.

I went upstairs and climbed up into my tree house. It's the best place in the world and even makes going to bed a treat. It was kind of odd really, as the tree house had been Holly's idea and Joe had designed it. They'd worked on it together and it had been built in a day while I'd been off on a birthday trip. It just showed how well suited they were. It was such a wonderful, wonderful idea. It was the best thing in my life. It was massive.

I lay on my back and watched my monkeys lounging around on the branches. Well, Funky and Hewitt were hanging by their tails. They're the sporty ones. Stinker just lay by my side, burping quietly. He's the brains behind the organisation.

'Stinker, I gotta problem,' I said in my gangster voice.

'Tell me about it,' said Stinker.

'I want to get Holly and Joe together. Holly's coming to babysit on Saturday. It's my big chance. But I don't know how to set it up.'

'S'easy!' said Stinker. 'Candlelight, soft music, a romantic dinner for two . . .'

'Well, three,' I said. 'I've got to be there too, unfortunately.'

'Candlelight, sweet music . . .' Stinker went on. 'And make yourself scarce after the dessert. Bring some up here for us. Eh, fellas?'

Funky and Hewitt agreed that a few tiny crumbs of some amazing pudding would be most welcome. I started thinking.

Candlelight? That was a good idea. Then Joe's spots wouldn't be so noticeable. I liked those scented candles you can get. Maybe a wonderful perfume drifting about would help. I wondered which scent they would like?

And then, music . . . ? That was a problem. Joe likes music so loud and heavy, it would be impossible to speak if that was playing. I wondered what sort of music Holly liked. If I only knew all the different sorts of music they were into, I might be able to get some that they *both* liked.

As for the dinner . . . that was also a challenge.

I'd never really noticed what sort of food Holly liked. And Joe – well, he can be really picky too. He's always changing his mind about things. He was a vegetarian for a week once. What chance did I have of organising a romantic dinner if I wasn't sure what food they both liked?

But I could hardly just ring Holly up and interrogate her about all this. I couldn't even ask Joe without making him suspicious. How could I collect all my information?

Suddenly I had a brilliant, brilliant idea. It was so brilliant I almost fell out of my tree. I'd make a questionnaire! I'd write a list of all the questions, and I'd ask everybody to fill it in – Mum, Dad, Yasmin, Zerrin, everybody – not just Joe and Holly. Then they wouldn't be suspicious.

I climbed down out of my tree house and ran to the PC in the study. I created a file called '?Air' (QuestionAir – get it?). These were some of the questions:

What is your favourite smell?
What is your favourite music?
What is your favourite food?
What is your favourite drink?
What is your favourite film?

I set it out on a page, leaving plenty of space for the answers. Then I printed out four for my own family. I was going to fill one in myself, obviously. I didn't see why I should miss out on the fun.

I e-mailed one to Yasmin and asked her to get her family to fill them in too. I said it was for a 'project'. Moments later, an e-mail arrived in my inbox from Holly, with the photos she'd taken of me with my monkey make-up on. What an amazing coincidence!

I whizzed back a reply saying how great her photos were, and how much I was looking forward to seeing her on Saturday, and asking her to fill in my ?Air. A reply came straight back:

'What fun, Ruby! I'll do it right now! Anything to avoid homework duty.'

I could hardly wait.

CHAPTER 10

You idiot! Why can't you ever do anything properly!

I TOOK A COPY to Joe and placed it on his head, so he had to grab it and take a look.

'Fill in my questionnaire,' I said. Joe sighed. He wiggled his fingers about.

'Gimme a pen,' he grunted. Wow! This was progress! I gave him a pen and a big book to rest the paper on.

'You don't even have to leave the sofa,' I said, to encourage him. Then I went upstairs. Mum and Dad were arguing (not horribly, just slightly) about where the chest of drawers should be.

'If we have it there, it blocks the way to the wardrobe,' said Mum.

'Well, if we have it over there, it blocks off the radiator,' said Dad.

'Hi, Mum, Dad!' I said, popping in with a saucy smile. I figured they needed distracting. 'I've got a questionnaire here. Please can you fill one in each? It won't take long.'

'Is it for school, love?' said Mum.

'No, it's just my own idea,' I said. 'I thought it would be fun to do some research.' The word *research* sounded quite important. I knew Mum would be impressed.

'Well, imagine!' said Mum, gazing fondly at me as if I was a genius. 'What a lovely idea, Ruby. Let's go down and fill them in for you now, love.'

'Yes, I've had enough of furniture moving,' agreed Dad. 'Let's put the kettle on.'

Soon my whole family were filling in the questionnaires: Mum and Dad at the kitchen table and Joe on the sofa. I took a peek round the door at Joe. He was laughing to himself as he wrote. Hmmm. I hoped he was taking this seriously.

'Oh, this is a lovely questionnaire, Ruby!' said Mum. 'But I just can't decide what my favourite

film is. I'm torn between *Some Like It Hot* and *Love Actually*. Does it matter?'

'Of course not!' I said. 'Put them both down. I don't care. I mean, I don't mind.'

It was sweet, the way Mum was taking it so seriously. And she didn't even realise that her answers were of no interest whatever. Although I would read them, obviously.

'I've finished,' said Dad. He handed me his sheet of paper with a kind of smug look as if he knew his answers were the most brilliant comedy. This was what he'd written:

What is your favourite smell? *Ruby cooking my dinner*

What is your favourite music? *Ruby snoring*

What is your favourite food? *Ruby's neck*

What is your favourite drink? *Hot chocolate spat in by Ruby*

What is your favourite film? *Easy Rider*

My dad is a bit weird, to be honest. He used to be a hippy and even played in a rock band years and years ago – which is why his answers were basically insane. I laughed a lot and punched him lightly on the jaw.

'Dad, you've ruined my questionnaire,' I said. But I wasn't really angry. As long as Joe and Holly filled in theirs properly, nothing else mattered.

'I've finished mine now too, love!' said Mum, looking pleased. This is what she'd written:

What is your favourite smell? *The smell of babies' heads*

What is your favourite music? *I'm very fond of Frank Sinatra, or jazz*

What is your favourite food? *Cheese salad with chips*

What is your favourite drink? *A cuppa tea when I get home!*

What is your favourite film? *Some Like It Hot with Marilyn Monroe*

'Thanks, Mum,' I said. 'That's brilliant!' She looked happy and I gave her a hug. What a pointless charade this all was. Still, never mind. I marched into the sitting room. Now for the real thing.

'OK, Joe. Let's have your questionnaire,' I said. He'd made it into a paper aeroplane and he aimed at me and launched it across the room. I grabbed it and read it:

What is your favourite smell? *Dead dog*

What is your favourite music? *Metal*

What is your favourite food? *Dead dog, lightly garnished with Metal*

What is your favourite drink? *The blood of goofy nerds, type 'O'*

What is your favourite film? *The Matrix*

'You idiot!' I snapped. 'Why can't you ever do anything properly?'

Joe gave me a sneery smile. 'Small Girl Loses Rag,' he said. 'Faint Shouting Heard Like Sound of Angry Flea.'

I went to the study. I was going to all this trouble to fix him up with the most glam girlfriend ever, and he just didn't deserve it. Maybe Holly had filled in her questionnaire by now. I went online and checked my e-mails. There was one from Yasmin.

'Hi Ruby! Great idea about the questionnaire. I've sent copies to Hannah and Froggo too. Plus I added some more questions – I've attached it so you can answer my questions too.'

'And you can kiss my monkeys' bottoms,' I said aloud. I didn't even bother to look at her flipping attachment. What a flaming cheek!

But wait! Another e-mail popped into my inbox. This time it was from Holly. I was so keen to open it, I almost deleted it. This is what it said:

What is your favourite smell? *Cinnamon . . . mmm, the smell of Caribbean islands, old fashioned chemists' shops, apple pies with cinnamon . . . Don't put undiluted cinnamon oil on your skin, though. I did it once and it stung for two days.*

What is your favourite music? *Right now I'm into Foul Play, but I could go off them just like that.*

What is your favourite food? *It's a problem . . . you see, I've decided to become a vegan. No meat, no fish, no eggs, no cheese, no dairy . . . what the hell can I eat? Nuts, I suppose. And fruit.*

What is your favourite drink? *It has to be spring water bottled in a place in Wales whose name I forget. I even wash my face in it. All other drinks are poison to me.*

What is your favourite film? *Amelie. I just love*

those quirky French films. Plus her haircut is to die for.

It seemed my attempts to organise a romantic evening were doomed. Holly and Joe were clearly totally unsuited to each other. I don't think you can get scented candles that smell of dead dog. And even if you could, vegans probably wouldn't be allowed to sniff them.

'So, how's the questionnaire coming along, love?' asked Mum perkily, poking her head round the door. 'Has Yasmin filled hers in yet? What did she say?'

I was beginning to wish I'd never started this.

CHAPTER 11
Don't try and boss us around!

NEXT DAY AT SCHOOL things got even worse. Yasmin came running up to me in the schoolyard waving a big envelope.

'I've made a huge questionnaire!' she shouted. 'We can get everybody to fill it in every time somebody new joins the gang! It's brilliant! I've done a copy for you – here you are.'

She opened the envelope and handed me a sheet of paper covered with questions. I was so tempted to screw it up and shove it down her throat.

'How many more people are you going to ask to join?' I asked, trying to sound sarky. 'Maybe we should invite the whole school.'

'Don't be silly, Ruby!' said Yasmin. She didn't seem to realise I didn't mean it and I was just having a dig at her. I glanced at the paper. There were questions like colour of hair, colour of eyes, length of hair, favourite colour . . .

'Sounds as if you're trying to find Ashcroft Primary's next top model,' I said in a sneery voice. Yasmin wasn't listening. She was looking around.

'Where's Froggo . . . ?' she said, half to herself. 'Ah, there he is!' She waved him over. Dan came over, doing a silly walk like a duck.

'I told him to walk like that,' said Yasmin, laughing. 'He's brilliant at it! Plus he does the most amazing quacks!' I was silent. Walking like a duck had been my idea. I had dared Yasmin to walk all the way home like that. She'd refused and instead she was now telling other people to walk like ducks, and pretending it was her idea. I was close to murder.

'Hi, gang!' said Froggo. 'Or should I say, *Zerrijo-hew-hah*!' He laughed and gave Yasmin the secret handshake. Then he shook hands with me too. 'What's wrong with you, Rubix?' he asked. 'Or

73

should I say – what was your name again? – Massive Poison Toad? You've got a face like a wet weekend!'

'A wet weekend! Ha ha ha!' Yasmin giggled. 'Where did you get that saying?'

'It's one of my dad's,' said Froggo. 'Listen, can Max join the gang? I've already taught him the handshake and the password. He wants to be called Fatal Killer Kitten.' Yasmin laughed again. She was getting into one of her laughing-helplessly moods. Usually it's one of the things I love about Yasmin. But now it just seemed totally stupid.

'I don't think we should have new members all the time,' I said grumpily. 'It's supposed to be a small secret gang, not a great big public thingy.'

'Well, just Max, then,' said Froggo. 'He can make some great noises. And he's got some fantastic ideas about horrid things we have to eat to show we're hard.'

At this point Hannah ran up waving a piece of paper. She did the secret handshake with everybody and then turned to Yasmin.

'I've filled out your questionnaire!' she said. 'It was brilliant. But I'm not sure what colour to call my hair. Would you say it was brown, dark brown, or chestnut?'

'Wait!' said Froggo. 'The password!'

'*Zerrijo-hew-hah*!' said Hannah, laughing.

'I don't think we should do the handshake and the password every time we meet,' I said. 'It's stupid. Anybody could overhear it. It's supposed to be secret. We should have special meetings of the gang and the rest of the time we should just be normal.'

'Don't try and boss us around, Ruby!' said Yasmin. 'Now we're a gang we can all decide how to run it.'

At this point I just snapped.

'It was my idea in the first place!' I yelled. 'You've just taken it over and you keep inviting everybody else to join in without asking me first! And you all keep changing everything! And you've stolen my questionnaire idea as well!'

'You're not the only person who can do questionnaires!' Yasmin yelled back. She loves a row. 'Anyway, your questionnaire was rubbish. It only had five questions. Mine's heaps better!'

At this point Max came running up with his arms outstretched. He was making an aeroplane noise.

'Can I join the gang, then?' he said. 'I think we should all eat the horrible things at lunchtime.

After our proper lunch. I think we should turn over stones and eat anything that we find underneath!'

I couldn't bear any more of this. I just walked away. As I went I heard them talking about me.

'What's wrong with Ruby?' asked Hannah.

'Oh, she's just in a strop,' said Yasmin. 'Ignore it. She'll be OK by lunchtime.'

I was determined *not* to be OK by lunchtime. All through maths and English, I tried to work out if I was being stupid or not. *I* had thought of the gang and the questionnaire, and Yasmin had sort of grabbed both of them and changed them completely without discussing it at all. My questionnaire hadn't really been anything to do with the gang, of course. It was just so I could sort of secretly find out about what Joe and Holly liked – what they had in common. (Nothing, as it had turned out.) But I still felt gutted. Of course anybody in the world can write a questionnaire. But the way Yasmin had sort of taken over the idea, changed it and then wanted all the credit for it made me sick.

The gang was my main problem, though. That really had been my idea. Yasmin had invited these others to join without even asking me, and now they all seemed to think they could do what they wanted.

Was it wrong of me to want it to be more secret and special? It would have been a lot more fun if Dan and Hannah had had to sort of apply to join the gang – and fill in a questionnaire and then be interviewed. Yasmin and I could have done the interviews and set them dares to do to prove they were brave enough.

So far I was the only person who had done my dare properly. And it had got me into deep trouble with Jenko. Yasmin still hadn't done a single dare. She'd wriggled out of the 'walk like a duck' dare, even though that was totally easy and non-threatening. No way would she have got into

trouble for walking like a duck all the way home.
We would just have had a big laugh, that's all.

I decided I was never going to speak to Yasmin
ever again, and at lunchtime I ate my pizza alone,
in a corner, facing the wall.

CHAPTER 12
I can't do this!
It's disgusting!

AFTER LUNCH I went out and stood in a corner of the schoolyard. I looked through the railings. There's a football field through there and some boys were playing football. Boys were playing in our schoolyard behind me too. I hated football. In fact, right now I hated everything.

Bam! I felt a great big bang on the back of my head. It jolted my head forward and my brow hit the railings. Somebody must have kicked a ball right at me. I just ignored them. I stayed where I

79

was and just went on staring through the railings as if nothing had happened. My forehead really hurt from where it had banged against the iron, but I was determined not even to rub it.

'Ruby!' I heard Yasmin's voice suddenly behind me. Then I felt her arm around my shoulders. 'Are you OK? I saw the ball hit you just now. That stupid Henry Young kicked it. I'll kill him.'

I just went on staring through the railings. Yasmin was right up next to me, looking in my face. I smelt her breath. She'd had falafel for lunch.

'Ruby, talk to me,' she said. 'I'm sorry we had that row earlier. I'm sorry if you don't want anybody else to be in the gang. But now they've joined I don't see how we can chuck them out.'

'You took everything over and acted as if it was your idea,' I said.

'No, it *was* totally your idea,' said Yasmin. 'It was brilliant. You have brilliant ideas. You're a *genius*. Please make it up with me. We can have our own secret little gang, separately from the rest of them, as well. What password would you like?'

'Monkey business,' I said half-heartedly. I didn't really want to be in another gang with Yasmin. I wished I was at home, in my tree house, with my monkeys, right now.

'OK, shake hands. Friends again, OK?' said Yasmin. 'You can have my piece of chocolate. OK? OK?'

We shook hands and she gave me the piece of chocolate. It wasn't a very big bit, but I suppose it's the thought that counts.

'Hey! Yasmin! Ruby!' we heard Froggo shouting. We turned round. 'Let's go down the field and do some dares!'

'OK!' yelled Yasmin. She grabbed my hand and we ran down to the bottom of the school field, where there's a bit of rough ground with a chain link fence and a row of trees.

We all sat down on the grass. Hannah and Froggo looked at me a bit warily. I smiled, but it wasn't a totally friendly smile. It was quite small and thin. We heard the buzz of an approaching aeroplane. It was Max.

'Can I join your gang?' he said, bombing us and machine gunning us on a fly past. Yasmin turned to him.

'No! Wait till tomorrow!' she said.

'But I've got loads of ideas about horrible things we can eat!' said Max.

'Oh, OK, then − if that's all right with you, Ruby?' Yasmin added. I just shrugged and sighed.

'Yeah,' I said. 'Whatever.' It seemed she couldn't say no to anybody. Max kind of landed beside us on the grass.

'I think we should all write a horrible thing on a piece of paper and pass it round,' he said.

'Yeah! Great!' said Hannah, flicking her hair about. (I ducked.)

'Sorry, folks, I haven't learnt to write yet,' said Froggo.

Yasmin got a little notepad out of her pocket and passed it around with a pencil. Each of us wrote something horrible. I couldn't believe we were just letting Max join in just like that. He hadn't done the solemn promise, he hadn't done the handshake or said the password. And he shouldn't even have known the password yet. Froggo should never have told him.

As each of us wrote something horrible to eat, we tore the page off the notepad, folded the piece of paper and put it on the grass in a little heap. Now it was my turn to write. I took the pencil and thought for a minute. I didn't even want to play this game. The thought of eating horrible things made me feel sick. So I just wrote: *EAT MY SHORTS*.

I folded the piece of paper and put it with the

others. Yasmin mixed them up so we wouldn't know which was which.

'OK,' she said. 'We each chose one and read it silently, and then we'll read them out loud.'

Dan took his piece of paper, read it and said, 'Ugh!' Hannah took one, read it and said, 'Urrrrrrgggghh!' Max took one and said, 'Yuk!' Yasmin took one and said, 'This is stupid!' Then it was my turn. I took one and unfolded it: *Eat a whole live worm.*

'I can't do this! It's disgusting!' I said and read it out to the others.

'That was my idea,' said Max. 'Mine says: *Eat somebody else's bogey.*'

'That was mine,' said Dan, looking foolishly proud of such a gross idea. 'I've got to eat a handful of mud.'

'That was my idea,' said Hannah. 'Mine is really disgusting. It says: *Eat a plate of dogfood.*'

'This must be yours, then, Ruby,' said Yasmin accusingly. '*Eat my shorts*? That's just totally stupid. I mean, it's impossible. Nobody could ever actually eat a pair of shorts. I mean, it's possible to eat a worm or some mud or a bogey or whatever, but you can't actually eat shorts.'

'You could cut them up and cook them with spaghetti sauce,' I said. 'But anyway, I think this game is just stupid and I'm not going to do it.'

'Go on, eat a worm!' said Max. 'If you don't do it, I'll do it, and then you won't be in the gang any more.'

'Don't you tell me I won't be in the gang!' I yelled at him. 'It was my gang in the first place! It's a stupid boys' idea to eat horrible disgusting things. The gang's not supposed to be about that anyway.'

'Well, if you don't do your dare you'll just be a scaredy cat!' said Yasmin. I turned on her

'How can you say that?!' I shouted. 'I already made a farting noise in silent reading and I got punished for that and everything. I had to stand by Mrs Wakefield's door for the whole lunch hour and I missed drama club! I've done my dare – and you haven't done one at all! Not even a little tiny harmless one. I am actually the *only* person in this gang who has *already* proved how hard she is, so the rest of you can go and take a running jump!'

I got up and ran off, back up towards the school. I went right indoors and straight to the library. We're allowed to visit the library in the lunch hour as long as we read and don't make a noise. I got a book out from the shelves and sat down and opened it. I just stared at the pages blankly. There seemed to be pictures of animals who lived in the sea, but I couldn't be sure. I wasn't even focussing.

When the bell went for afternoon registration, I put the book back and went to our classroom. I sat in the far corner and pretended to look for something in my bag. I was determined not to look at Yasmin and the rest of them when they came in. I really was *never* going to talk to them again. *Really*, this time.

'Ruby! Put that book away and pay attention!' Mrs Jenkins sounded in a foul mood. I put my bag away and sat up straight.

Mrs Jenkins began to call the register. I answered

my name and stared at my hands. I was determined not even to look at Yasmin and co. But wait! Yasmin wasn't there! Nor was Dan. Nor was Hannah. Nor was Max.

'Ruby!' Mrs Jenkins was frowning at me. 'Where are Yasmin and Hannah? And Dan and Max? Were you with them at lunchtime?'

'No, miss,' I said. 'I was reading in the library.' It had such a saintly sound. I could almost feel my halo shining softly above my head. A bit like a small portable patio heater.

'You were *not*!' hissed Angelina Brookes. 'I saw you with them on the field!' She's a bit of a snake in the grass. I gave her a sneery look. Mrs Jenkins hadn't heard.

'They were down at the bottom of the field when I last saw them, miss,' I said, just to be on the safe side. 'I wanted to come in so I went into the library. Mrs Gordon saw me there.'

'All right, all right,' said Mrs Jenkins. She was looking a bit worried. But at that very minute the door opened and Hannah came in.

'I'm sorry I'm late, Mrs Jenkins,' she said. She had been running and she was out of puff. 'But Yasmin – we were down at the bottom of the field, and Yasmin's been sick.'

'What about Max and Dan?' she asked. Hannah blushed and looked embarrassed.

'They're a bit sick too,' she said. 'They've gone to the medical room.'

'Did they all eat the same thing at lunch?' asked Mrs Jenkins, looking puzzled. Hannah blushed again and looked sheepish.

'No – it wasn't that. The thing is, please miss, they were eating worms,' said Hannah. 'We had to do it for a dare. Only I wouldn't.' Mrs Jenkins heaved a very big stern sort of sigh and glared at Hannah.

'Sit down,' she said. 'I've never heard of anything so silly. Right, get out your history books. Today we're going to find out about the pyramids. Find page twenty-four.'

Hannah sat down in a guilty sort of way. I ignored her. Normally I feel sorry for people who get ill at school, but this time, somehow, I didn't feel sympathetic at all. Quite the opposite, in fact.

CHAPTER 13

I thought she was a Martian

NEXT DAY YASMIN didn't come to school. She's often away. Her mum fusses like a mother hen if Yasmin's ever ill. Hannah, Dan and Max came to school as usual, but they sort of avoided me in the yard. There were certainly no secret handshakes or passwords. It was as if the gang had never existed.

'Do you think Yasmin's really ill?' said Hannah to me at lunchtime. I shrugged.

'I don't know,' I said. 'And I don't care.'

'Are you going to ring her tonight and find out how she is?' asked Hannah.

'No,' I said. I liked the way I was sounding quite hard and grim. Almost gangsterish, in a way.

'Why not?' asked Hannah. 'Aren't you best mates any more?'

'No,' I said again. 'Yasmin and I are history.' And I stood up and carried my dirty plate off to the plate rack. I could feel Hannah watching me as I walked out. It was a good feeling. As if I was in control for the first time for ages.

I really didn't phone Yasmin that night. There were no text messages from her and no e-mails. I certainly wasn't tempted to send one myself. There were other things to think about anyway. Next day was Saturday, and Holly was coming to babysit.

I whizzed a text off to Holly to remind her. A secret horrible dread crossed my mind for a moment. What if Holly had forgotten about babysitting and had fixed to do something else?

DON'T FRGET BBYSTNG TOMORO, my text said. Right away, a reply came back: *WDN'T MSS IT FR THE WRLD. CU 6.30? LOVE, HOL. X*

Saturday passed very quickly, because Mum went shopping to buy herself a dress to wear to the retirement dinner that night. She dragged me along for advice.

'Does my bum look big in this, Ruby?' she asked, struggling into a sage green number. I looked up from my Game Boy. I wasn't sure what to say. Her bum looks big in almost everything.

'. . . No,' I said, but my voice kind of wobbled a bit.

'I know what that means,' said Mum in a disappointed voice. 'What about this pale blue number?' I shrugged. How could she expect me to be interested? I am a gangster-to-be, after all. She should have had a daughter like Yasmin. I bet Yasmin is her mum's style adviser.

'Yeah, try it,' I drawled.

I was annoyed that I had thought about Yasmin. I had decided to wipe her out of my memory banks. Totally and utterly. I returned to my Game Boy. I was already on level four. But Mum had told me to turn the sound off. She always insists on that in public. So I sort of have to play the soundtrack in my head.

'I quite like this pale blue one,' said Mum, zipping it up and smoothing the front down. I looked up. It was a loose style and it looked heaps better.

'Brilliant,' I said. 'It really suits you, Mum. Get it.'

Mum looked pleased and a bit embarrassed at all my flattery. She turned this way and that, anxiously staring into the mirror. Finally she decided that I was right. This was definitely the one.

'It's funny, really,' she said thoughtfully as we queued up to pay for it. 'I've never worn pale blue before. Well, not since I was a girl. You don't think it's too young for me, do you, Ruby?'

Secretly I was convinced that pale blue was way too young even for me. But I just wanted her to stop talking about clothes.

'Mum, it's perfect,' I said. 'Can we buy something special for supper tonight? I mean for me and Joe

and Holly. Holly's a vegan.' Mum looked startled for a moment.

'That's a special kind of vegetarian, isn't it?' she asked.

'It's a vegetarian who doesn't eat dairy products either,' I told her. 'Or eggs. Basically they won't eat animals or anything that came out of an animal.' Briefly I thought of Yasmin and Dan eating worms down on the school field, and for a moment I was almost sick myself. It was enough to turn anybody into a vegan.

'Sounds like it'll have to be a salad, then,' said Mum, paying for her new dress.

I nagged her into buying the ingredients for a really massive and wonderful salad before we went home. I *so* wanted Holly to have a good time with us.

For the rest of the day I tidied my room. Holly always likes to visit the tree house and sometimes my room gets so messy, there is just no carpet left to walk on. The only problem with having a tree house is that you can't hide things under the bed. I always used to do that. Now I have to put them away properly, which is a bore. But this time I was so excited about Holly coming I didn't really mind.

I was glad I'd given up the idea of trying to arrange a special candlelit supper for Holly and Joe. It was way too much stuff for me to organise. And besides, it might be better just to let things happen in their own way.

Everything had turned out just perfect with my other big problem: the gang. I hadn't had to plan a revenge or anything. It had taken care of itself. I was beginning to feel lucky. I had this feeling that Holly and Joe would just hit it off this evening, without scented candles or sweet music or anything special at all.

After all, last time Holly had come, Joe had got changed, and he'd smelt much nicer when he'd come down again after going up to his room. OK, Holly had left in the meantime, so he'd missed her. But that was just bad timing. Tonight they'd have the whole evening ahead of them.

When I'd finished in my room, I went back downstairs and started to wash the salad. This is the most boring job in the world, but because I was doing it for Holly it didn't seem so bad. I would hate her to find a bit of dirt on a lettuce leaf, or be faced with a cheeky slug chomping through her cucumber.

The idea of a slug reminded me of Yasmin. I

wondered if she had really completely eaten the worm – swallowed it and everything. Or maybe she had just put it in her mouth and spat it out? Either way, I had to admit Yasmin had guts even to think about doing a thing like that.

I sort of wanted to know all the details. Although, in another way, I never wanted to think about it ever again. I wasn't going to think about Yasmin either. She really must be wiped from my memory banks. But it would take some time.

Joe came into the kitchen and stared over my shoulder into the sink, which was full of water and lettuce leaves. He grinned.

'Terrible Wreckage After Hurricane Doris,' he said. 'Whole Rainforest Trashed. All Monkeys Drowned.'

I hit him, because the thought of monkeys drowning was designed on purpose to upset me. But I didn't want to launch a full-scale row because I wanted him to be in a good mood for Holly, so I didn't hit him very hard. I also needed, really subtly, to remind him that she was coming.

'This is for Holly's supper,' I said. 'She's coming to babysit tonight. She's a vegan.'

'I thought she was a Martian,' he said, moving away and opening the fridge. He scanned the shelves. I couldn't tell what sort of expression was on his face: whether he was thinking of Holly at all.

'You can have supper with us if you like,' I said. 'You don't have to have salad. You can have whatever you like. Bring your own dead dog.'

'Stuff that,' said Joe. He got a can of drink out of the fridge and then shut the door in a careless, harsh kind of way. 'I'm going out.' And he slouched off upstairs.

I felt totally crushed. But maybe it was just one of his lies. Maybe he'd just said that so I'd think he couldn't care less, whereas actually he *did* care a whole lot? Maybe he'd gone upstairs to shower and change and put on fresh fragrant socks? Maybe he would go out, but only down to the corner shop to buy some cool aftershave?

After all, even if he was crazy about Holly and desperate to see her again, he'd hardly admit it to his little sister, would he?

Ten minutes later, Joe came downstairs. He was wearing better clothes and he smelt nice. My heart gave a little skip. So he was interested in Holly after all! He'd made a real effort –

'I'm off out, then,' said Joe. He strolled off down the hall and seconds later I heard the front door shut with a horrible dull thud. I couldn't believe it! He really *had* gone out! He didn't like Holly enough even to be here when she arrived! My heart sank down into my trainers. I felt really, really terrible. Holly would be arriving in a minute. Could things possibly get any worse?

I looked down dolefully into the sink. Aaaaaargh! A horrid slug was really in there! Floating about on a lettuce leaf! A small grey slimy one! I almost screamed aloud. I ran off to find Dad and ask him to deal with it. This was a clear message from the universe: *yes, Ruby, things can get worse.*

Little did I guess just how much worse they were going to get . . .

CHAPTER 14
Look at you now!
Amaaaaazing! Hahahahahaha!

ABOUT TEN MINUTES after Dad released the slug out into our back garden, the doorbell rang. I ran to answer it. It was Holly. She looked utterly amazing.

'Hi, Rube!' she grinned, tripping lightly inside. She tapped my nose with her finger as she passed. I couldn't help smiling, although really, on the inside, my heart was heavy as lead.

Holly was wearing a completely fabulous black dress covered with various zips. She had on lacy black tights and wonderful black and white boots. Mum came into the hall, pulling on her coat.

'Oh hello, Holly,' she said. 'We're just off out. Ruby's planned a salad for you to share – I hope that's OK?'

'Salad's my favourite,' said Holly.

'You look very stylish, love,' said Mum. 'I like your boots.'

'Thanks, Mrs Rogers,' said Holly. 'You look fabulous too.'

'Oh no, do you think so?' said Mum, coming over all awkward and anxious. 'Ruby helped me choose this dress. But I'm still not quite sure about the colour. This pale blue . . . it doesn't seem quite right somehow.'

'It's beautiful!' said Holly. 'You look amazing. The blue goes with the blue of your eyes. Emma Thompson was wearing a dress like that at a premiere the other night. You look like a million dollars!'

Mum looked pleased and confused. She never knows what to do with compliments. I was pleased that Holly had made her feel better about her dress. Then Dad came in.

'Come on, old girl,' he said. 'Or we'll be late. They'll be tipping the pig food into the troughs as

we speak.' Typical of Dad's approach to a romantic
dinner dance.

Mum and Dad left, and Holly and I went into
the kitchen. Holly's make-up was brilliant – her
eyebrows were like a couple of wild Japanese
brush-strokes and her cheeks kind of gleamed as if
golden powder had been dusted on. She looked
full of fun. Her eyes were sparkling and dancing.

*She must be wondering when Joe's going to come
down,* I thought. *Shall I tell her he's gone out?*

But somehow I just couldn't. If I told her he'd
gone out, then it would seem as if I thought she
was coming round specially to see him. And even
though I was sure she was, it would be rude to say
so. Or something.

What's more, I couldn't face seeing the light die in her eyes when I pronounced the awful words, 'Joe's gone out'. And she looked so glamorous and everything. She'd so obviously made herself look good just for him. I mean, nobody gets all glammed up just to go babysitting, do they?

'Can you help me with the salad?' I asked. 'I'm hopeless at cooking.'

'I don't think salad has to be cooked for very long, Rube,' she laughed. 'About half an hour in a hot oven should do the trick.' She took the lettuce and the tomatoes and everything and chopped the cucumber into cute little sticks. I watched. Her fingernails were painted bright red. Her fingers are long and amazingly quick. My hands are hot and pudgy and as clumsy as anything.

'OK,' she said. 'I'll just make a dressing. Do you like dressing? Some kids don't, I know.'

'Oh yes!' I said. 'I love it!' I was lying, though. I don't really like dressing but I didn't want to disappoint her.

'Do you mind a bit of garlic in the dressing?' asked Holly, reaching for the garlic squeezer.

'No, fine!' I said. To be honest, I find raw garlic a bit fierce. It gives you breath like a lion. But if Holly wanted it, that was fine.

'You lay the table,' said Holly, adding all sorts of strange little things to the dressing: a pinch of sugar, a dash of mustard, a swirl of black pepper. A bit like a magic spell.

I got out two plates and put them on the table. This was the moment when she'd realise Joe was out – or at least, that I didn't expect him to eat with us. She glanced over her shoulder at what I was doing and I saw the exact moment when she clocked the two place mats, the two plates, the two table settings. Just for a split second she hesitated and there was a tiny, tiny moment of darkness in the air. Or was it my imagination?

'Right,' she said, bringing the salad to the table. 'What could be nicer than this? A cosy little supper for two. Shall we have it by candlelight?'

'I don't know if we've got any candles,' I said. It was ironical, really, because of course I'd been planning to have candles for the romantic supper for her and Joe.

'There's some over there,' said Holly. 'On top of the fridge.' She went across to fetch them. 'And afterwards,' she went on, 'we can snuggle up on the sofa and watch that French film I told you about – *Amelie*. I've brought the DVD with me.'

'What's it about?' I asked, as she arranged the candles on the table.

'It's about this fabulous girl who falls for somebody,' said Holly, 'and by being amazingly clever, she sort of creates lots of puzzles and mysteries for him, until he's desperate to know who's behind it all, and – oh, you'll just have to see it for yourself. Where are your matches, Ruby?'

Suddenly there was the sound of a key in the front door. We both froze for a moment. The dinner was set, the candles were almost lit – could it be that the romantic supper was on after all?

'It's Joe,' I said. For a moment a smile crossed

Holly's face, and her face sort of lit up. Then, suddenly, everything changed. There was the sound of giggling out in the hall. A *girl* giggling.

The front door slammed shut, and we heard somebody came down the hall towards the kitchen. It seemed to take for ever, like a slow-motion sequence in a film. Then Joe appeared in the doorway, with a stupid grin on his face. Standing next to him – well, standing practically inside his jacket, *with her arm round him*, was a girl I recognised from the Dolphin Café near the high school.

'Hi!' said Joe. 'Vegan Feast Ruined by Gatecrashers!'

'Hahahahahahah!' giggled the girl.

'You know Tiffany, don't you?' said Joe in an off-hand, rude kind of way. 'Tiffany – Holly.'

'I know you by sight!' said Tiffany. 'Who wouldn't? I mean – you always look amazing! Look at you now! Amaaaaazing! Hahahahahahaha!'

'Hi,' said Holly crisply. 'Want some salad? There's plenty.'

'No, thanks,' said Joe. 'I never touch salad. I don't do green.'

'Hahahahahaha!' giggled Tiffany. I wanted to kill her.

'We're going upstairs to watch my *Batman Returns* DVD,' said Joe.

'OK,' said Holly. 'Have fun.' And she turned away to get us some glasses of water from the sink.

Joe and Tiffany lurched off upstairs, laughing at nothing. Holly was standing with her back to me. I couldn't see her face, and I didn't really want to. Poor Holly! This was the worst evening of my life!

'Right, Ruby,' said Holly, coming back to the table and smiling a smile that was just slightly too bright. 'I've thought of a fun way to eat our supper. We've got to eat it as if we're characters in a murder mystery.'

The way I was feeling, if I found myself alone in a room with Tiffany for thirty seconds, we *would* be characters in a murder mystery.

CHAPTER 15
Yeah . . . Whatever

IT WAS QUITE HARD to eat the salad, for some reason. But I forced it down. It was a clever idea of Holly's that we should eat as if we were in a thriller. It made it easier. She was very good at it. She sort of nibbled at the leaves in a suspicious way as if she thought I was trying to poison her. It was almost fun. We would have laughed a lot if it hadn't been for the soundtrack of *Batman Returns* blasting out upstairs.

'Want some ice cream or a yogurt?' I asked when we'd finished the salad.

'No, thanks,' said Holly. 'They've both got milk in, and I can't eat milk because I'm a vegan.'

'Oh yes,' I said. 'I think I might become a vegan too.' I hadn't had much of an appetite this evening. And it seemed that vegans were hardly allowed to eat anything. So right now it suited me just fine.

We cleared away and loaded the dishwasher, and then we started to watch *Amelie*. It was hard to concentrate, though. Even with our sound turned up quite loud it couldn't compete with Batman's vile noise upstairs. And *Amelie* wasn't a loud film, it was sort of feathery and light. Almost like a fairytale.

My other problem was that it was all in French. It did have subtitles in English, but I can't read very fast. Halfway through the film, Joe's door burst open and he and Tiffany clattered downstairs.

'So much for Batman!' he said through the open door. 'What's that you're watching?'

'*Amelie*,' said Holly.

'Oooooh!' said Tiffany. 'SO arty!' Holly ignored her.

'We're off out, then,' said Joe. Holly shrugged. Her eyes never left the screen.

'Yeah,' she said with a shrug. 'Whatever.'

After Joe and Tiffany had gone, the evening seemed sort of hollow. I tried to concentrate on *Amelie*, but I couldn't, and after a while I said I was going to bed.

I lay awake for a long time, wondering what Holly was thinking, on her own, downstairs. I hoped she wasn't too upset. I hated boys, and I decided there and then that I would never have a boyfriend when I was older. Not even one who looked slightly like a monkey.

Next day was Sunday, of course. Mum announced that she wasn't going to be cooking Sunday lunch because she and Dad were still suffering the after-effects of their dinner the previous night.

'I'm going out anyway,' said Joe, and in an instant he was gone. I hadn't told Mum and Dad about Tiffany coming round last night. I wasn't going to either. I wanted to pretend even to myself that it hadn't happened.

'I don't want a big Sunday lunch anyway,' I said. 'I'm not hungry.'

I went to the computer and looked for e-mails. There was nothing from anybody. Then, suddenly, my mobile buzzed. It was Holly.

'Hi Ruby!' she said. 'Listen! I'm in town and I've discovered there's a brilliant show on this afternoon at the theatre. It's Roald Dahl's *The Witches*. There's a matinee at half past two. Would you like to come? We could have lunch first in the bar. It's my treat.'

'Wow!' I said. 'Great! I'll ask Mum and ring you back.'

Mum and Dad didn't seem to mind at all. In fact, they seemed quite pleased to get me out of their hair. I had a feeling they were going to have a very long siesta this afternoon and a couple of aspirins each.

'Just give Ruby a lift into town, Brian,' said

Mum. Dad agreed. And even though Holly had said it was going to be her treat, they gave me £15 for my lunch and my ticket.

On the way into town my phone buzzed again. It was a text message from Holly. *GUESS WHAT*, it said. *I'M NOT ALONE. SOMEBODY HERE TO MAKE UP A 3 SOME. MYSTERY GUEST! XCITING OR WHAT? LOVE HOL X*

Suddenly the most brilliant idea flashed into my head. She was going to be there with Joe! They had met up somewhere and they'd got together, just like I'd always hoped and prayed they would. They were together after all! My heart was pumping with excitement as Dad dropped me off outside the theatre and I went up to the café bar.

It was really crowded, and being small I couldn't see through the throng of people. But then somebody moved and I saw Holly standing up and waving. I pushed my way through the crowds towards her. Any minute now I was going to see Joe, sitting there and looking a bit embarrassed but pleased in a sort of boyish way. I just knew he was going to say one of his headlines.

'Local Artist Takes His Little Sister to the Theatre – Shock Horror,' he would say. '"Too Scared to Watch Witches Thing Alone," He Confessed.'

At last I reached Holly's table. But Joe wasn't there at all. It was Yasmin! She was sitting next to Holly and looking a bit embarrassed.

'Sit down, Ruby,' said Holly. 'Next to Yasmin,' I obeyed. Yasmin was sitting on a kind of bench thing. 'Zerrin's getting us some juice. Will that be OK?' I nodded. Zerrin was standing at the bar. She waved to me.

'And we've ordered pizza,' said Holly. 'I've decided I've been a vegan for long enough.'

'Fine,' I said. It felt really weird sitting next to Yasmin again. But kind of nice.

'Yasmin's got something for you,' said Holly. Yasmin handed me a pink envelope decorated with hearts and ponies. I opened it. Inside was a home-made card with a picture of a girl looking rather like Yasmin, with two long black bunches of hair and wearing a pink skirt. Two big tears were rolling down her cheeks and in huge sparkly letters it read *I'M SORRY*. She had signed it 'Luv, Yas' and drawn about fifty kisses underneath. Holly must have helped her make it. No way could Yasmin have made such a cool card on her own.

'Nice card,' I said. 'Thanks.'

'I am sorry, Ruby,' said Yasmin. 'Really sorry. I was horrible.'

'OK,' said Holly. 'Now shake hands and be friends again, or I won't love you any more.'

We shook hands. Secretly, Yasmin gave my hand three squeezes. She winked at me. I winked back.

'Best friends again?' said Yasmin. I gave a gangsterish smile and a shrug.

'Yeah,' I said. 'Whatever.'

It did feel really nice and cosy though, being best mates with old Yas again.

After the show (which was brilliant) I went back to have tea at Yasmin's, because it was her granny's last day in England and she wanted to hug and kiss me to death before she went back home. Yasmin's mum said they had missed me. It felt so good to be back.

That night as I lay in bed, I thought how odd it had all been. I had wanted to get Holly and Joe together. But in the end Holly was the one who got me and Yasmin back together.

'There's just one problem, though, guys,' I said to the monkeys. 'I still have to get Holly together with Joe. But Joe's so blatantly going out with Tiffany now. How am I ever going to manage it?'

'Shuddupa yer face!' said Stinker. 'I'm trying to sleep.'

'Anyone for tennis?' said Hewitt. He's got a one-track mind.

'Tomorrow is another day,' said Funky, trying to be helpful. I suppose he's right, really. I went off to sleep straight away and dreamed I was a witch.

When I woke up I couldn't decide whether to be a witch or a gangster when I grow up. I'm going to have to ask Mrs Jenkins for some careers advice. One thing's certain. I'm never ever going to be a marriage guidance counsellor. I'm leaving that sort of thing to Holly.